This book belongs to

_____

**Do Babies wear pyjamas?**
**Written & illustrated by Fransie Frandsen**

Copyright © Fransie Frandsen, 2022

First published in 2022 by artfox.bookwolf
Text and illustrations by Fransie Frandsen, www.fransiefrandsen.com
Design and layout by Gregory Page, www.pigment.ch
Editing by Sandra Bialystok, www.sandra.bialy.ca

ISBN 978-0-9568287-4-3

It was almost bedtime, and Alexander was already in his pyjamas

and ready to go to sleep.

Alexander looked at Baby T who was trimming the Tinster's hair.

**Mummy stopped what she was doing and looked at Baby T.**

"Do babies wear pyjamas?" wondered Mummy.

**She was not at all sure.**

# Not

# at all sure

Alexander immediately decided to help Mummy find the answer to the puzzling question:

Do babies wear pyjamas?

**Daddy couldn't hear very well as his ears were full of soap.**

# Full

# of soap

**Mummy and Alexander spotted the neighbour in his garden.**

"I have a question about pyjamas," shouted Mummy.

**The Tinster had buried the neighbour's pyjamas in his garden the week before.**

still

looking

The next afternoon at school,

"Surely, such a thick book will have all the answers about babies," thought Alexander.

# He found information about:

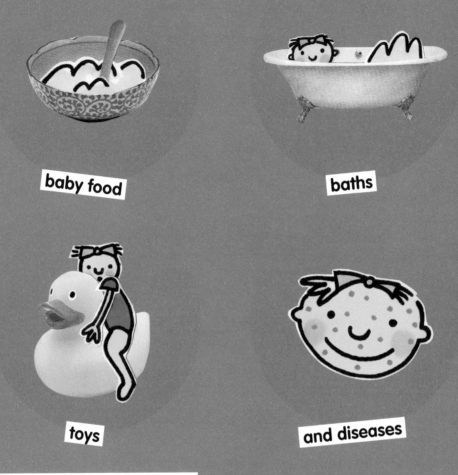

baby food

baths

toys

and diseases

## and even facts about:

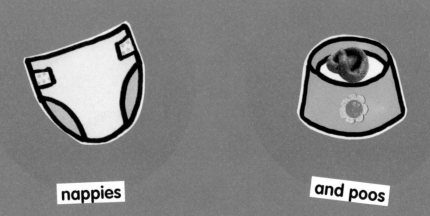

nappies

and poos

## but absolutely no answers to the question…

# Do Babies wear pyjamas?

**By now, it was getting late**

"But what on earth was she going to wear?" worried Mummy.

# What

# on earth?

who was camping somewhere in the middle of Africa.

The telephone connection was so bad that Mummy had to shout.

"Do babies wear pyjamas?" yelled Mummy.

**Mummy's sister could not hear very well,
as just at that moment,
lions were roaring outside her tent!**

Instead of hearing the word "pyjamas", Mummy's sister heard "bananas".

And thinking that Mummy was looking for a recipe with bananas...

# Mummy's sister shouted recipes for:

banana milkshakes

banana muffins

banana jelly

banana smoothies

banana curry

and banana cupcakes

# and then continued with more recipes for:

baked bananas

and banana jam

**Mummy stared out the window at the early evening stars.**

**Alexander had never seen Mummy looking more worried.**

# Never more

# worried

**And they all immediately rushed off to Baby T's room.**

The moon was shining brightly outside Baby T's window. And the stars were peeping through the curtains.

**Alexander peered into Baby T's cot and whispered:**

"See Mummy, babies don't need pyjamas."

**As Baby T had already drifted off to sleep...**

...and was dreaming of lions
in fluffy pyjamas,

sipping sweet
banana milkshakes.

**Do Babies wear pyjamas?**
**Written & illustrated by Fransie Frandsen**

**About the author**
Fransie Frandsen is an artist,
writer and art therapist.

She is keen on words,
mad about markers,
bonkers about books and thinks
kids are completely cool!

Fransie has lived in six countries,
has five four legged friends,
speaks four languages,
holds three qualifications,
loves her two children, and shares
her house with one husband.

Fransie now lives and works
in Switzerland.

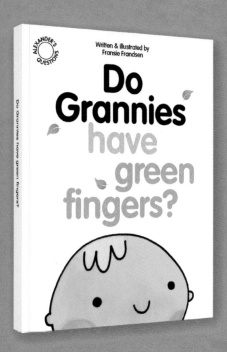

ALEXANDER'S
QUESTIONS

Written & illustrated by
Fransie Frandsen

# Do Grannies
## have
## green
## fingers?

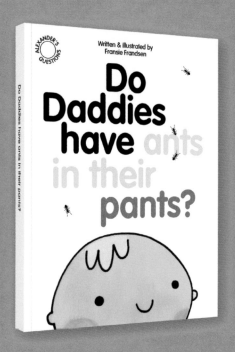

ALEXANDER'S
QUESTIONS

Written & illustrated by
Fransie Frandsen

# Do Daddies
## have ants
## in their
## pants?

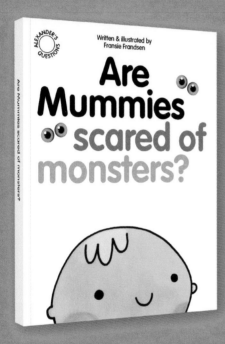

ALEXANDER'S QUESTIONS

Written & illustrated by
Fransie Frandsen

**Are Mummies scared of monsters?**

Are Mummies scared of monsters?

ALEXANDER'S QUESTIONS

Written & illustrated by
Fransie Frandsen

**Do Babies wear pyjamas?**

Do Babies wear pyjamas?

Titles in the Alexander's Questions series